Lust, Love, and Memories

Yolanda Santa Cruz

ISBN: 978-1-7364948-0-6

I will always make time for
emotions, and that's how this
book came to be.

Contents

Lust

On connection

Sex is just easy with you.

My orgasms come quietly,
inadvertently,
like a summer breeze
that blows up the curtains
in a country house,
allowing you to see
the beautiful landscape outside.

So in tune you are with my body
that you notice it rising even before I do.
And you stop to let me enjoy the mountains,
and the flowers, and the birds.

At my own rhythm,
on my own pace.

And this makes all the difference,
to say the least.

Playground

He told me
I was his favorite toy.
I replied
he was a good kid.
At least he didn't break me
after a bit of playing.

He said
that's what you do with toys
if you want to keep using them
for a very long time.

Phallocentrism

Yeah, I mean,
some things you can't replicate.
No matter how much you fall for others
with the same intensity
that you gave yourself to him.

When I write about this
I'm not talking about anything deep,
nothing spiritual, nor magical:
I'm being quite petty and shallow.

I'm talking about his cock,
and the way I can't use it
in any other act
with any other actor.

Which is quite disappointing and tragic.

And that's that.

Just another thought

What if our safe word is
I love you?
That would make shit get deep
real quick...

Common ground

I think we would both agree
it's scary how well we get along.

...but no rush

The things I want to tell you
are losing meaning and relevance
and my desire to see you
is following the same path.

Sneaky Pete

Stop sliding into my DMs.
I don't need you,
and most importantly:
I don't want you.

Lia

I thought of you today.
Fucking in the college dorm
with everyone hearing your
moans from across the hall.
Everyone talking about how
loud they were.

And it hit me,
for the first time,
how sad it was
that I will never know
what you sounded like.

Desire

I prefer to die
knowing I was wanted
than to live
feeling like an extra.

Grandview thoughts

I need you to desire me.
That's just the way it works.

I can't lie in bed with you
if I'm not sure you badly want
to feel your cock
slowly entering
the warmth of me.

I need to rest assured
you are counting the days
until you lick my pussy,
over and over,
with steady pressure,
just the way I like it,
right until I come.

That you wake up hard
dreaming of my mouth
tightening around you.
Driving you crazy
in a way you said
you no longer realize
what the hell I'm doing.
And how so great it feels
you are dying to come
but your body won't let you

'cause it wants to feel more.

I don't think you crave that
-not as of now-

Desire is combustible:
If it doesn't burn
then there is no flame.

So, I prefer not to see you.
I prefer not to have you.

We were too good together
to settle for
mediocre sex.

Casual

Do you think you can do that?

I was born casual, babe.
But fair enough,
that's the kind of question I get
for being so fucking caring.

Wet dreams

I've fucked you
so hard
in my dreams,
I don't even
want to fuck you
in real life
anymore.

Recovery

I don't find myself daydreaming
about your cock anymore.

So, I guess that's a win.

Full of fire

How can you like The Knife
and not be good at fucking?

I don't see a logical scenario for this.

Reality check No.2

Babe,
I think you got confused.

You thought
I was really your toy.
Available to please you
whenever you felt like it.

You failed to realize
it was just roleplay.
A very fine one,
but nonetheless, a game.

#whatashame

Fuck

Is all you say.
You don't realize
the more you say it
the less you get it.

I know it troubles me

Must be hard to focus
while having me in your head
all the time.

I fucking want you
inside me again.
It is not a statement.
It's a fucking order.

- Universe, comply. -

Hard to meditate

At present
I feel warmth in my belly.
I press my thighs together.
I want you down there.

I get hot listening to Radiohead
with our red bedroom lights,
dreaming of tomorrow.

You see?
Even when I focus on the present,
I keep living in the future.

Vanishing

Tactile memory is so ephemeral.
I need you
to keep reminding me
the way your hands felt
while grabbing my ass.
Your fingers
entering slowly
the dark between my thighs.
The way your mouth was
full of saliva
whenever you decided to kiss me.
While I begged you
blindfolded
quietly, and in Spanish.

Body scan

You said my fingernails
left trails over your skin.
Next time I'll have to go deeper
as I didn't see any of them.

Meeting more frequently would do too.

Play no games with me

I see through your actions
your attempts to break me.
I'll give it to you straight:

Don't waste your damn time.

I've got a Masters in sociopathic behavior.
5 years of training with a thesis included.
It wasn't a course you just take and forget.

The teacher still tests me
every now and then.
I no longer fail.

So, get straight to the point.
Play no games with me.

Cock-tales

Why the fuck
am I so obsessed with your cock?
Is it because of how nice it was,
or am I trying to convince myself
the only reason I keep writing about you
is it because the sex was too good?

But keep trying

Like an egg
you are trying to crack me,
but I'm hard-boiled already.
So even if you succeed
it's not going to be
what you are hoping for.

Exchange

I would exchange my soul
for a cigarette right now.
In any case, I don't think I have it
at this moment.

Wasted

We used to be a playground.
Now we are a litter box.

Afterthoughts

I just came hard
and my first thought was:

What a shit show.

I bet you masturbated
today at your place too.
Thinking about last Friday.
Exactly a week ago.
Exactly around this time.

We were creating art.

But you are a jerk.
Or afraid of your feelings.
Or God knows what the fuck.

So here we are.
Apart.

Love

Plain and simple

I think you are just afraid
of falling in love with me.

My two cents

She has two lovers,
so why can't you?
Her reaction is not fair,
I know that you know it.

But it is not my place
to spotlight this fact.
After all,
she might be your excuse
to get away from us,
because in reality you can't bear
the burden
of again falling
for someone already taken.

Børns

The emotion was,
suddenly,
out of me.

To you,
the emotion was melancholy;
to me,
it was desire.

I hear the song
and all that comes to mind
is that I was in an orgy
full of sexy people,
with my eyes wide open.
With lights that looked like the future.
With people devouring me.

There, I realized,
it was out of me.
I left it in your room
that same morning.

What they were looking for was,
suddenly,
out of reach.
And that was the emotion to me.

Unspoken words

I had to bite my tongue with you
so early on.

I didn't see it coming.

The only time I felt something similar
was for someone with way more history
than what the two of us had.

Full rage mode

I don't want to focus
on what's good in my life.
I don't want to be grateful I had you.
I don't want to channel
any fucking positive thoughts.
I had you.
I saw you tremble over me.
I felt electric charges
while your fingers ran over my skin.
I felt the connection.
I was there;
you were too.
We had something I had never seen.
You saw me raw.
You saw me as comfortable
as I have ever been.
You,
motherfucking coward,
decided to step out of it all.
I can't focus,
I won't focus,
on what was good about us.

Desynchronized

I was waiting on your text
like a Christmas present.
Didn't realize
summer had just started.

Wetness

I don't care if I need to use lube
for the rest of my life.

I'm texting you
no more.

My unrequested texts

I just feel silly.
Silly and ashamed.

I try to love me.
I try to respect me.
Instead,
I kept texting.

I keep reaching out,
even when I say
I won't do it again.
Even when I say
there is no reason to text.

Shouldn't be that hard
to stop writing him.

Inaction
shouldn't take
this much energy.

Act accordingly

Your actions
don't bother me.
They just set the mood
for future interactions.

The mud pool

I feel that finding each other
was like stumbling upon
a gold nugget
in a pigs' mud pool.

I was the pig
frolicking in and out,
definitely not looking for
any gold in there.
What were the chances
anyway?

I just wanted a good
'ol fashioned
childish highschool crush.
Something
to keep me coming back
to the barnyard every day.

But then,
there was us.
More than a childish crush.
More than a sexy distraction.
More soul than weightlifting body.

And I guess I just wonder
if you,

muddy, dirty pig,
feel the same way about us.

And so fucking far away

No Facebook,
No Instagram,
No VK.

I guess all I really have left
to know about you
will be just my dreams.

Skipped WOD

Something was a bit off today.
There were no thrusters,
but there was no you.

And I wondered
where you wandered.

How my poems are created

Whenever
I want to write you
I write me.

Overnight

The way he holds me
while we are asleep
as if
I were his property

it makes me feel
I've found an owner.

4 walls and a mattress

You make me feel like a teenager
all over again.
With your bed on the floor,
seeing your belongings
piled up on your shelves.
Having to be quiet because of your roommates.

It's painfully beautiful how much
it gets the best of me.

Of my sweet afternoons,
carefree of time and future.
When I focused on the present,
which was the only thing we had.

Not lost in translation

So, I say:
Tu ne me manques pas
and even Google Translate recognizes it.

I'm not great at French, you see?
Most times,
when I say something to Google
it only catches one-third of it,
if anything.

But this,
this it understood clearly.
I only had to say it once:
Tu ne me manques pas

I think the confidence in my voice
the way I made it sound,
like it actually existed,
like it was somehow corporeal,
made Google realize
it was a statement.

and my dry vocal variety
made it correctly guess
what the hell I meant to say.

Fact

If you are dancing
next to a couch's leg
you can't say
you weren't looking
for a hurt little toe.

WhatsApp messages

You bury yourself when
you don't write to me.

Public Park

I was at this public park
in San Francisco,
the one next to the Pier
with the floor of stones.

The sky was so blue,
The weather just chilly enough
to make you appreciate
the warmth of our Sun
There were seagulls crying,
and butterflies flying.
I was lying on a bench,
contemplating
Perfection.

That's when I knew
you weren't the one,
because,
even though I missed you,
I didn't care
you weren't there to feel it all
and I didn't care
about telling you either.

Contemporary tales

He watches my stories,
I watch his.
I watch his stories,
he watches mine.

It just feels like
freaking Morse code.

Unfriend

I'm always going to be there for you.
That's why I prefer not to be.

@andreeaverde

Cute, beautiful, gorgeous
she is.
With her blue hair,
silky outfits,
and red lipstick.

She is a living example that
you can be
the three of them.

Sometimes even
simultaneously. 🖤

Can we talk?

I am not ready to talk to you.
Just the thought of it scares me,
but I don't like that feeling anymore.

Tonya

I feel
so Tonya
sometimes.

Trashy,
tempered,
bold.

Trying to
fit in
without
entirely
losing
myself.

I thought about you yesterday

Love, don't lie to me.
You have thought of me
way more than just that one time.

Question

Maybe it is true.
Maybe you don't think of me as often.
Could it be that?

I know you like to play games.
Also, I do know you respect yourself.
I wonder which is the reason
I'm not getting a response.

Are you really not feeling it?
You don't want to appear weak?

For the last reason, there is no need, love,
I'll like you no matter how weak you are,
no matter how small I get.

As for the first one,
I like you anyway.
I just need to know your why.

Toast

I propose another toast.

This time
for all those things that we post
thinking about someone
we know will see them,
and we know will like them,
but they won't
"Like" them.

Because reality is a bit more complex,
and this is a good example.

During sex

I felt like saying
I love you
but I didn't
'cause I told you
sane people don't do
these sorts of things.

Now I feel like
sane people
don't know what
they are missing out on.

Friend-portrait

My friend tells me I'm like a mojito:
Sweet, bitter, fresh, and harsh.

She knows me too damn well.

Spring

When the sun makes you cry
'cause it's been a while
since the last time your eyes
saw it so bright.

Thoughts

I'm scared I'll never get bored of you.

Reality check

Sorry,
I'm not sorry.
I know, such a cliché phrase.
But,
Don't you think
you deserve it?
Crossing lines like
there were no risks
in the field.
I'm an open field,
but I'm mined.
Never forget that.
Everything in me
can be seen and reached,
at first glance.
That doesn't mean
you can run me over.

I'm going to implode inside you,
tearing you to pieces,
because you ran me over
without caring to see
what you were stepping on.

Unconditional love

Jesus will keep loving you.
No matter how fucked up
and creepy
you think he is.

Red lights

Illuminate this paper.
There is no way
I'm going to look at
red lights
the same way anymore.
Not after you touched me
the way you did
under them.

Practical prayer

Please oh lord I beg you,
allow me to respect myself enough
to be able to keep him.

At sunset

The Sun doesn't set, the Earth shies away.

In contrast, drama comes like a breeze

Happy moments don't want to come out.
We don't want them to.
We want to keep them contained within us
for as long as possible.
That is why it is so hard to write about them.

On feelings

My feelings don't worry me.

I worry about the present
and not enjoying life.

I worry about
not having feelings.

So, every emotion is welcome.

Le Soliel

I do think you take us seriously, and you think of me often / But you know / You know space is important / You know damn well about energy flows / That's how you can feel me coming so well, after all / In the same way, you know I'm peeling off my skin right now / I'm sunburnt red / Waiting to heal, slowly, after exposing so much of myself to you / So you are giving me time before you touch me again / And I can only thank you for that / Had it been up to me, even though I felt like I needed it / I would have gotten 3rd degree burns with you / just to end up disfigured after us.

Within

We were walking by the street,
he was caressing my neck.
I was resting my arm on his back.
We were going at a slow, steady pace.

It had all the ingredients to make
my effortlessly romantic heart
believe we are a couple.
Yet, it didn't feel like it.

I still don't know why,
but it's been haunting me.

Lovebird

Love. Lovebird.
What do you see in the desert?

There is no food out there.
The nights are long and cold.
The Sun hits like if you were
in a pot of boiling water.

What's so compelling about
miles and miles of nothingness?

What is it, love?

Could it be the feeling you get
when you actually see something
peaking on the horizon?

Maybe it's better than the city in here
with everyone passing by
but nobody noticing one and other.

Perhaps I should move
to your desert after all.

State of mind

I just don't wanna see him again.
Just.
Don't.

#universeyouhaveopenenedyourears

You seem way too normal
at being a freak
way too organic
way too soft
and darling
softness is my soft spot.

Coincidence

I feel like talking to you today,
but I don't want to reach out because
I don't want you to think
it's a February 14th kinda thing.

Silent love

We keep becoming
quieter and quieter
while making love.
I have the feeling it is
because there are words,
scary words, according to society,
that we don't dare to say.
So, we stare at each other
every time more in-depth
and for longer periods.
As if wishing that
our eyes could do all the talking.

But they are falling short.

Bodies are just containers

It never felt so true
than when ours got together
and their content blended in so well.

Lightness

You are free now,
feel the weight of it.

Trust

You had no time for us.
That's what you said to me.

I chose to believe you
because it's less painful
to be rejected by you,
than to think of you as a coward.

9/1/20

I keep telling myself it was just a matter of time, anyway. In two months from now, I was going to leave the gym, the area. We were going to stop seeing each other as often. Things would dilute and one day would turn into 3-5 without communicating.

We were going to drift apart. It was coming. It was just a matter of time.

I do want to believe this, but I know it is so fake. Convenience has nothing to do with love and desire. They don't even know each other. When one enters a room, the others have already left… or were never there.

I know it would have worked, until it didn't. Having to drive 10 minutes more to fuck with you was not going to be the reason.

So, I have to sit with this uncomfortable uncertainty of not knowing how it could have ended, because we didn't get to that point. I guess I should call this "the point". Definitely not your typical movie ending. No drama involved. No lack of feelings. No resettlement. Maybe I should be grateful for parting on such good terms, with such a good memory of our last love-making session. With your 3 climaxes and my over 30 orgasms. Some people have it tougher.

I guess it is true: even the bad things that happen
in my life, happen in the best possible way.
I have so much more to write about this. But the
page is ending, and I don't know if it's worth it
to turn the page to keep crying over spilt milk.
If I turn the page, it won't be for that.

Memories

Memories

Some memories stay with you
like shattered pieces of a broken glass,
making you bleed
every time you stumble upon them.

Search

When I lose my center
I go back to my writers.

They are rarely
the famous
the dead
or the established.

They are mostly
young women
I've found via Instagram.

I pick up their books.
I read one by one
every dog-eared page,
every sentence highlighted.

They remind me
in a close,
warm way,
that I'm not alone.

I can make
something powerful
out of uncertainty.

Nightfall

Hard to be
under
the same sky,
looking at
the same
cloud formation,
just about
3 meters apart,
knowing
I no longer
belong to you.

Free writing

Sometimes
writing
down
your emotions
is enough
to
validate
them.

How ironic

I keep
blasting out
the song
you used to hear
while healing
now that
I'm in pain.

My emotions

I won't tell you how I feel.
You will think I have no emotions.

Truth is, my hands bleed out
as I write down on these papers
all the things I want to tell you
that you won't ever know.

Broken words

Bella, linda, yolinda,
favorite toy,
favorite student.

I bet you won't reuse
these words.
They will linger
in your vocabulary,
lacking functionality.

Just like
broken words
that can't be
thrown away.

Emptiness

Our chemistry is pretty amazing.

He said,
as he walked away.

Unstable

He loved birds,
but was afraid to fly.

I have my art

If anything,
I have this.

I just want to throw myself into my papers.
Write with the two of my hands
until my wrists start hurting,
'cause I'm hurting,
and I see no better way
to take this pain out of me.

Consistency

He treated his emotions
like all his profile pictures,
hiding every expression
behind dark-tinted shades.

Life in confinement

You are so important in the story of my life
I grew tons thanks to us.
Your presence, your behavior,
our interactions, the emotions I felt,
the way I had to channel them
made me learn a lot about myself.

I'm aware
how difficult it must be
to put yourself in my position
and understand what I'm saying.
I'm aware it is like talking to a prison wall
that has no idea how much its limitations helped
you to reach within.
How the confinement made you stronger
prepared you for loneliness, silence,
and longing of freedom.
How much it roused your imagination
to daydream about spring days in a field full of
flowers,
being able to walk for as long as you wanted
towards the horizon in any direction.
Scenery that you knew you would never witness,
but that was the only way to keep your sanity in
the dark and cold of your isolated cell.

You gave me all that.

Your bricks,
so compact and rigid
allowed me to create
my own perception of freedom.
One that I carry with me everywhere I go.

And now that I think about it,
this might not be that hard
for you to understand.
After all,
I bet you had your own walls too.

Inspiration

He doesn't know
he is going to make me famous
with his absence.

Doorway

I was standing at
the same door
where I once told you
I liked you,
but this time
I left before you did.

Ig

Seeing that our last conversation was 10w ago breaks my heart into pieces.

Hurt

My head keeps visualizing
the pictures
we could have taken.

While listening to Estopa

Learning to live with the memories of you
is one of the toughest things I have had to do.

Chin-chin

I propose a toast
for that chemistry between humans
everyday harder to find,
that we still, somehow,
manage to impale
once we have it in front of us.

Driving

I saw through
the rearview mirror
the dark,
uphill road
getting smaller behind me.
And
I thought,
in that second,
that I was leaving the city
and I was leaving you.

Pieces

You might appear normal,
but you are broken.

And there is no way
to reverse that.

Remembering

I remember when I used to think
my eyes had superpowers.
Remember those times?
What a waste we have become...

About dreams

Even good dreams are nightmares in the end,
once you wake up to reality.

L'adieu

You didn't come with a problem,
you came with a solution.

You had already decided
too many things were on your plate.
I was the easiest one to take out,
perhaps the least messy of them.

You just wanted to let me know.
Like an infomercial.

Had you come to me
with the problem,
I would have fought for you.
You would have heard my fury.
My incomprehension over
her double standards,
and your willingness to comply.

I would have asked you
at least a few questions:
What bothers her the most?
Would it be better if she meets me?
What's too much time for you?

Your problem could have taken
so many routes.

Yet, what you were presenting
was your definitive solution.
One that you determined
after two weeks of thinking.
And to that,
I don't have much more to add.

So, I say:

We had great chemistry,
and I will miss you babe.

Little poem

The life
and the flies.
Life flies.

Current situation

Yawning
so they don't notice I'm crying.
Sleeping
so I can stop the thinking.
Emptying myself
slowly and by the drop.

Like a fig
hoping that at least
what's left has a sweet taste.

Nostalgia

I'm so tired of
re-reading
our conversations
from 3 years ago.

Wild life

I remember how we made each other feel.
It was wild.

I still get images of the two of us
out of the blue sometimes.
There's an "ahh" sound that inevitably escapes
between my lips every time I do.
Sometimes it sounds raspy, corroded,
like rusty metal.
I can hear the pain passing through my throat in
the form of air.
Sometimes it is sweet and short
like the sight we get while looking at a beautiful
landscape very early in the morning.
Sometimes the images are so intense that my
whole body spasms.
My eyes close instinctively.

Those times I get chills because
it was wild,
but it was wildest
to let us go.

Consolation prize

Maybe,
one day,
we will get back together.

Perhaps,
that day,
your hair will be long again.

(that will make it worth the wait).

And that's the way it was

A totally tumultuous and discolored relationship.
Everyone we knew was part of it,
except ourselves,
right until the end of it.

Still here

You still appear in my browser history
at least once a month.

No, we didn't want to walk at 7am

No one does that just because of the art of
walking.
No one walks 2 hours straight after not having
slept the entire night.

Even less without the time to do so,
with only half a cup of Cuban coffee in our
system.

With a thesis awaiting me;
with a seminary awaiting you.

I don't write this to convince me,
I write this because it bothers me
to realize it now.

7/4/18

I discovered today
I'm not strong enough yet
to mark down your YouTube videos
as "not interesting content".

Liberté

vuela
pájaro libre,
ya bastantes poemas
te he sacado.

Nothingness

Not having you by my side in bed.
Not running my fingers around your shapes.
Not feeling your silky skin.

Like a waterbed
without interior decor.
Like a notebook without
its pages.
Like a self-sterile plant.

That's how it feels.

The one-night stand

I imagine, one day in the future, people learning
that we were together. They will probably say
something along the lines of "Oh, really? I never
noticed" "Must have been a one-night stand, or
something like that" "Nothing too serious, in any
case".
I imagine them, simplifying what the two of us
had. Stripping emotions out of their sentences.
Reducing our story to just a body exchange.
Like we only existed as two separate objects that
turned into a five-minute gossip when placed
together. As if our talks, our walks, our texts,
our pictures, our videos, our connection, had
never existed.
And maybe it isn't that important. Any of that.
Maybe I'm the one taking us too seriously.

Author's Note

I have been able to find myself in a lot of writers. Through their poems, I have gotten the sense that my feelings are valid, even those that are not so welcome. I want my book to be one of these safe spaces for others as well. I want you to read it and know that it's ok, whatever you are going through, and even learn to appreciate all of your feelings without holding back out of fear of what could happen if things don't go the ideal route. It's okay. You are not alone, and like I wrote in one of the poems: you can make something powerful out of this.

If you have something to share, I will love to hear from you. Find me on Instagram @yolanda_santacruz_